This book is dedicated in loving memory
to my grandfather, Ernie Boyd.

Journey of the Freckled Indian: A Tlingit Culture Story

This book was made possible by the Native Arts Grant from the Potlatch Fund (www.potlatchfund.org).

Book design: Monica Rickert-Bolter

ISBN: 978–1–7342863–0–4
LCCN: 2020903247

Culture Story
511 Jordt Circle
Anchorage, Alaska 99504
323 379 9420
www.CultureStory.co

Publisher's Cataloging-In-Publication Data
(Prepared by The Donohue Group, Inc.)

Names: London, Alyssa, author. | Rickert-Bolter, Monica, illustrator. | Singletary, Preston, 1963- illustrator.
Title: Journey of the freckled Indian. [1], A Tlingit culture story / story by Alyssa "Yáx Ádi Yádi" London ; illustrated by Monica Rickert-Bolter ; Northwest formline designs by Preston Singletary.
Other Titles: Tlingit culture story
Description: Anchorage, Alaska : Culture Story, [2020] | Interest age level: 007-012. |
Identifiers: ISBN 9781734286304 (paperback) | ISBN 9781734286311 (hardback) | ISBN 9781734286328 (ebook)
Subjects: LCSH: Racially mixed children--Juvenile fiction. | Tlingit Indians--Alaska--Social life and customs--Juvenile fiction. | Grandparent and child--Alaska--Juvenile fiction. | Heredity--Juvenile fiction. | CYAC: Racially mixed children--Fiction. | Tlingit Indians--Alaska--Social life and customs--Fiction. | Grandparent and child--Alaska--Fiction. | Heredity--Fiction.
Classification: LCC PZ7.1.L662 Jo 2020 (print) | LCC PZ7.1.L662 (ebook) | DDC [Fic]--dc23

Journey of the Freckled Indian

A Tlingit Culture Story

Story by
Alyssa "Yáx Ádi Yádi" London

Illustrated by
Monica Rickert-Bolter

Northwest Formline Designs by
Preston Singletary

Foreword

Actual front page of Juneau Empire, with a headline in the Tlingit language. Tlingit áyá xát means "I am Tlingit." This is an important statement about your identity in a Tlingit introduction about who you and your people are. This front page of the newspaper (from Tlingit country) was one of the few times that the headline was written in the Native language.

Tlingit áyá xát

(Klinkit eye-ah hut)

"I am Tlingit"

It is important to know yourself and your cultural background. Having a strong sense of identity helps build confidence and pride in your heritage. It also can fill you with a sense of purpose to be an active part of your community.

Blood quantum is a relatively new and foreign concept to Native communities. This concept defines who is and isn't considered Native by their percentage of ancestry. But it was not the way of Native people to say we are "part" something. Blood quantum teaches that someday our children's children will not feel the right to claim their culture.

Most of us these days are part of many different cultures and have a diverse heritage. The Journey of the Freckled Indian book helps families and teachers facilitate conversations with children about identity.

As the saying goes, and the book's theme, "If you don't know where you come from, it is hard to know where you are going." Having regular conversations about identity at an early age helps kids grow up with higher self-esteem. With more confidence, children develop stronger skills and abilities inside and outside the classroom.

When you celebrate all aspects of the cultures that make up your heritage, you get to define your identity and instill a sense of purpose. Each part of your culture is yours to own and claim.

There once was a young girl named Freckles.

3

At recess, kids made fun of her.

They would say, "You don't look like an Indian, you have freckles. Real Indians are brown and have long black hair. You don't look like that at all."

The little girl was sad and cried on her way home from school.

Later that night, she twirled her spaghetti with her fork at dinner. Her mom and dad knew something was wrong.

Her mom lovingly asked, "What's wrong, Freckles?"

"The kids made fun of me and said I don't look like an Indian," Freckles responded.

Her parents looked at each other in agreement and nodded. Her dad said, "It's time to visit Grandpa in Alaska."

Freckles flew on a big jet to Ketchikan, Alaska. When she arrived, Grandpa greeted her with a big hug and said, "Tlingit áyá xát!"

"What's that mean?" asked Freckles.

Grandpa replied, "It means 'I am Tlingit' in your own language."

"But I don't look Tlingit," she said sadly.

Grandpa chuckled, "Come with me."

7

On their way to the seaplane, they drove past Saxman village.

"Look out the window at the totem park," Grandpa gestured.

"Grandpa, what are those? Painted trees?" Freckles looked curiously.

"They are carved and painted cedar logs, my dear," said Grandpa.

"I want to see them up close!" she exclaimed.

They stopped and walked through Saxman Park to admire the totem poles.

"The totem poles are one way that our people communicated our stories and passed down oral history," Grandpa explained.

"Wow!" Freckles said. She was so excited to be learning about her culture.

After visiting the totem park, she and Grandpa flew on a small seaplane that landed on Prince of Wales Island.

Freckles and Grandpa explored the island.

"Grandpa, what's that squawking sound?" asked Freckles.

"Oh, that's just Eagle and Raven arguing," Grandpa said familiarly.

"They sound so funny!" she giggled.

Freckles and Grandpa hiked to the river. It was so FULL of fish that they could almost walk across on top of them, like a fish bridge.

Freckles and Grandpa saw a boy using his hands to scoop the fish onto the riverbank.

"Hey! How do you do that?" she asked.

The boy said, "Like this!" And he effortlessly showed her how.

She scooped both of her hands, put them in the water, but slipped on the wet rocks, and scared all the other fish up the river.

HE HE

HE HE

The Eagle and Raven laughed at her.

"I will never be a real Tlingit," Freckles pouted, looking down at her feet.

"Hey you!" said a voice from afar.

"Who said that?" she asked.

"I know what you can do!" Raven proclaimed. "If you catch the biggest fish, you will finally be a real Tlingit."

Eagle shook her head and said with concern, "Oh Raven, what are you getting her into?"

Freckles felt encouraged.

The next day, Grandpa took Freckles fishing.

Freckles felt like they had been trolling around in the open water for hours when she felt a bend in her rod.

"Grandpa! I think I got something!" Freckles yelled.

But the pull grew **stronger** and **stronger** as the reel spun *faster* and *faster* as the sound of the uncoiling line grew LOUDER and LOUDER, and the spool went out farther and farther until it yanked her out of the boat into the cold... open... ocean.

Once Freckles realized what happened and opened her eyes, she was face-to-face with the biggest fish she had ever seen! The Fish blew a bubble around her to help her breathe.

She gasped, "What's happening?!"

"You tell me. *You* thought you could catch *me*, the biggest fish in the sea, and that would make you *Tlingit*?"

"Well yes, that is what Raven told me," she said.

"You can't catch me! I am not just any fish. I am Fred *the* Fish, the biggest *King Salmon* of them all!"

"But I have to bring you to Eagle and Raven to prove that I'm a 'real' Tlingit. Please let me catch you!" she begged.

Suddenly, Killer Whale appeared out of the shadows. With a regal, booming voice, she said, "You already are Tlingit. It is just who you are. No one can take that from you."

Fred the Fish wiped his brow and grinned, "Well, that lets me off the hook. Hehe! See you around, Freckles!"

As he swam off, she could hear Fred singing, "Remember, if you don't know where you come from, it is hard to know where you are going..."

As Fred disappeared into the distance, Killer Whale turned back to Freckles, "Don't let anyone challenge who you are. It is up to you to decide that. Stand strong because you know your identity."

And with that, Killer Whale lifted Freckles back into the boat with a powerful blast from her blowhole.

She landed gracefully back on the boat next to her grandfather, who did not look the least bit surprised. She and Grandpa shared a knowing glance and hugged one another.

Back on land, Grandpa had a big surprise for his Freckles.

He gave her Tlingit regalia and a silver eagle bracelet. Both of them had happy tears in their eyes as she stood there wearing it for the first time. She felt so proud to be Tlingit.

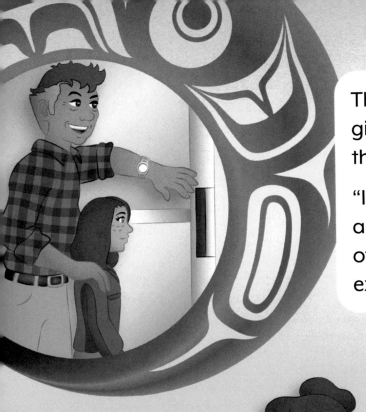

The next day, Grandpa brought the little girl to one of his favorite restaurants, the Pioneer Café, in Ketchikan.

"I wanted to bring you here to look around and see all the people. Many of them are of mixed heritage like you," explained Grandpa.

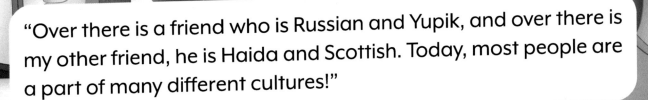

"Over there is a friend who is Russian and Yupik, and over there is my other friend, he is Haida and Scottish. Today, most people are a part of many different cultures!"

Grandpa continued, "My point is that just because someone has more than one heritage, it doesn't mean they belong any less to any one part. Each part makes them who they are."

Freckles nodded and, in a peaceful tone, said, "Yes, Grandpa, each part of my heritage makes me who I am. Now I understand."

"You just have to own all parts of who you are and where you come from, and be proud of it!"

Grandpa hugged Freckles and continued, "Your freckles represent the diverse heritage that makes you, you. That's why you are my Freckled Indian, my proud Indian girl at that."

She kissed her Grandpa on the cheek and grinned, "Yes, Grandpa. I am your proud Freckled Indian!"

Back at school, Freckles felt confident and was not nervous when her classmates approached her to ask where she had been.

"In Alaska with my Grandpa. I learned more about my tribe," said Freckles joyfully.

"Your tribe?! Come on, Freckles, you aren't really a part of a tribe," one laughed.

"Yes, I am. Tlingit áyá xát. That means 'I am Tlingit.' And no one can take that away from me," she proclaimed with the certainty of Killer Whale. "Do you know *your* heritage? Do you know all the cultures that *your* family members come from?"

Her classmates looked at each other confused.

"Well, if you don't know where you come from, it is hard to know where you are going," said Freckles with a cheeky grin. "Who you are in part comes from your family's heritage and is not necessarily just about how you look."

Her classmates looked curious and inspired. They turned and started asking about each other's cultures.

With a twinkle in her eye, like Raven by the stream, she skipped merrily away with an unshakeable sense of confidence from knowing who she is.

About Alyssa London

Author

Photo by Matthew Crockett

Alyssa London is an Alaska Native Tlingit, which is a tribe from Southeast Alaska. She also has Czech and Norwegian heritage from her mother's side. Her mixed ancestry is why she is fascinated with cultures and the concept of identity. *Journey of the Freckled Indian* is Alyssa's first published children's book with the intent to spark conversations between parents, grandparents, and educators with children about their identity. She also hopes to increase people's understanding of modern Native people. Through the book and her efforts with her company, Culture Story, she strives to educate Native and non-Native people alike about the vitality of Indigenous cultures and interconnectedness of people from diverse heritages worldwide.

Pictured right: Alyssa in the middle with her mom and her dad, Debi and Tate, in 1990.

Pictured far right: Alyssa, Tate, and "Fred" the fish.

About Monica Rickert-Bolter
Illustrator

Monica Rickert-Bolter is a Chicago-based visual artist of Potawatomi, African American, and German descent. Passionate about storytelling through art, she advocates for cultural representation in any project she undertakes. Monica brought the *Journey of the Freckled Indian* book to life as the illustrator, graphic designer, page layout designer, and copy editor. The book took form through her talent, dedication to the project, and ability to work collaboratively with Preston and Alyssa.

Photo by Benjamin Bolter

About Preston Singletary
Northwest Formline Artist

The art of Preston Singletary, Tlingit, has become synonymous with the relationship between European glass blowing traditions and Northwest Native art. Preston contributed the Northwest Coast Formline artwork to *Journey of the Freckled Indian*. The imagery in the background, as well as several of the characters, came to life because of his contributions to the project. The book would not be as grounded in Tlingit culture if it were not for Preston's willingness to contribute.

Photo by Julien Capmeil

29

Made in the USA
Columbia, SC
13 October 2020